Sophie Washington
Secret Santa

By

Tonya Duncan Ellis

Other Books by
Tonya Duncan Ellis

Sophie Washington: Queen of the Bee

Sophie Washington: The Snitch

Sophie Washington:
Things You Didn't Know About Sophie

Sophie Washington: The Gamer

Sophie Washington: Hurricane

Sophie Washington: Mission: Costa Rica

Table of Contents

Chapter 1

You've Got Mail

"Jingle bells, Batman smells, Robin laid an egg!"

"Be quiet, Cole!" I put my hands over my ears to muffle my brother's out-of-tune singing and focus back on my laptop to finish my English essay. It's less than three weeks until winter break and my teachers have been piling on the assignments to make sure we get our end of semester grades in.

There sure is a big change between fifth and sixth grade, workwise, at Xavier Academy, the private school my brother and I go to. Between all the essays and projects and studying for final exams, I feel I can barely take time to pat my dog, Bertram, when I get home; whereas, my eight-year-old brother Cole acts like he's already on vacation.

Since we got home from school an hour ago, he's been living it up, shooting hoops in the driveway, eating a snack and now playing on the handheld video game player that my mother would make him put up if she were downstairs with us. I ought to tell on him now...

Ding Dong!

The doorbell interrupts my thoughts.

"Can you get it, Sophie?" Mom yells from upstairs. "I'm putting some clothes in the closet."

I would ask her why she wants me to answer the door, and not Cole, but I already know the answer: "Because you're the oldest."

Of course, that logic doesn't hold when it comes to who gets the first dessert or who doesn't have to do the dishes at night. As the baby of the family and favored child, my little brother has got it made.

I trudge to the front door in time to see the mail carrier heading back to his truck. He's left a medium-sized box on the porch. *Wonder what it is?*

My mother sometimes has holiday packages delivered to the house, but Cole and I haven't made our Christmas lists yet, so I doubt it's anything for us. I open the door, pick the package up, and check out the label. It's got my name on it in bright, red ink, "Sophie Washington."

Who could this be from?

I never get any mail, except for birthday gifts my Granny Washington sends to our house in Houston from Corpus Christi when she can't be here, and I don't remember my parents ordering anything for us online. Granny is driving up to see us tomorrow, so I doubt she would mail presents here when she could just bring them with her.

"Mom, I got a package!" I call out.

"What is it?" Cole bounds from the family room to stare at the box as I set it on the kitchen counter.

"Back off, Cole, it's mine," I move him to the side with my hip and take a closer look at the delivery. The box is wrapped in brown paper, and there is no return address. It looks difficult to open with my fingers, so I pull a butter knife out of a drawer in the kitchen and slit through the tape on the side. A sweet, sugary scent fills the air.

"Cool!" exclaims Cole in appreciation as the brown wrapping slides off to reveal a box filled with packages of licorice, gummy bears, gum, and red and green M&Ms. I notice a typed note underneath.

Dear Sophie,

Hope your day is super sweet!

Your Secret Santa

Chapter 2

Secret Santa

Secret Santa? Who could that be?

"They didn't say anything about having any holiday parties in my homeroom," I say to myself. "That's just for the lower grades."

I remember participating in a secret Santa gift exchange a couple of years ago in my fourth grade music class. It was fun to pick the name of a classmate from a red and white furry Santa hat and then secretly give him or her presents throughout the week. We couldn't spend more than ten dollars. I chose my best friend Chloe. It was easy to find presents a prissy girl like her would want, like hair bows, fancy socks and other girly girl things. My Santa, a boy named Franklin Ruel, didn't try to figure out what I would like and left boxes filled with gooey gummy worms, superhero comic books, and baseball cards at my desk. He might as well have bought me a bag of coal.

"It's probably from one of your boyfriends," says Cole, picking up the discarded box while chowing down on his tenth gummy bear.

"Would you stop eating all my candy!?" I complain, scooting the gift box away from his grubby fingers. "I won't have any more left."

"Both you kids need to put the brakes on the sweets," says Mom, "or else you might get stomachaches. Why don't you leave the rest of that up in the pantry?" she suggests, handing me a wicker basket to dump the candy in.

"I can't think of who would want to be my secret Santa," I say as I'm putting up my treats. "We aren't doing a gift exchange at school, and no one has said anything about having any holiday parties."

"I told you, it's one of your boyfriends," Cole says and puckers his lips, makes kissing noises. "Nathan Jones has liked you since the spelling bee last year. And what about that other new boy who moved here from Ohio… Tony?"

"His name is Toby," I say, shrugging my shoulders. "And they both are my friends. I don't have or want a boyfriend."

"That's right, Cole," echoes Mom. "No one around here is old enough to have a boyfriend or girlfriend."

"You're the one who all the little ladies are after because of your basketball skills and your super fine 'fro," I tease, rubbing his thick curls.

Cole brushes me off, picks up his video game, and starts playing. "I don't like any of them because they're all ugly!"

"We'll see what you say about that a few years from now," my mother laughs.

The next day at school, I can't wait to tell my friends about my surprise package. I zigzag my way through the crush of bodies, elbows out and head down, so no one stops me. As usual, Mariama Asante, Chloe Jenkins and Valentina Martinez are hanging out near my locker before class. We are all members of the cheerleading squad and the best of friends.

"Slow down, Sophie! All that schoolwork isn't going anywhere," jokes Toby Johnson, flashing a dimple and putting his arm on my shoulder to keep me from ramming into him.

"Sorry, Toby," I blush. "I wasn't watching where I was going."

"No worries," he says, then waves and heads off the gym to play basketball with the other boys before the bell rings for homeroom.

I walk over to my friends.

"Cute kicks, Sophie," Chloe, ever the fashionista, says as she admires the new navy shoes my mother gave me this weekend as an early Christmas present. She usually buys Cole and me just three gifts, like the Magi got in the Baby Jesus Bible story, but my old school shoes had a huge hole in them so she caved and bought me something extra this time.

"That is so neat, Sophie!" exclaims Mariama after I announce the secret Santa news. "We didn't have anything like that in my country."

Mariama moved here to Houston from Nigeria last year. She celebrates Christmas, but I guess they do some things different over there. When she first came to our school she was really shy and sad that she didn't have many friends, so Chloe and I let her join our dress-up team during Homecoming spirit week. Mariama's mother made us long, colorful African dresses called 'boubou' to wear that everyone loved. She's been in our friend group ever since, and we all tried out for the cheerleading squad together earlier this year.

"I wonder if your Santa is somebody from our class?" whispers Valentina, looking around the hall. "Did the package have any other information in it?"

"Just a short note that wished me a super sweet day," I reply.

"'Super sweet,' maybe it's from a boy!" Chloe exclaims, twirling around.

"Sounds like someone has a mucho grande crush on you, Sophie," adds Valentina. "Toby was certainly eyeing you when you were coming down the hall."

"Yeah, I saw him put his arm around her," Chloe chimes in.

"That's because I almost knocked him over," I say, blushing. "Besides, everyone knows Toby likes you, Chlo."

Here we go again. Since a few months ago everything has been about boys with those two. I guess it's not hard to see why. They are the most popular girls in our grade. Tall and model thin, Chloe has dark curly hair and smooth caramel skin, and Valentina, whose parents are from Mexico, is funny, bubbly and cute.

"It could be from a boy or a girl," says Mariama, changing the subject. "I say 'super sweet' all the time. Will you get other gifts?"

"When we did Secret Santas in fourth grade we gave presents every day of the week," Chloe says. "But I've heard of some people who just give one Santa gift."

The warning bell rings and she stops talking. The hall swells with kids rushing to class.

"Gotta go," says Valentina, picking up her backpack. "I was late to homeroom last week, and I don't want to get another tardy."

"Tell me about it," I answer. "I've already been late to homeroom twice this term, and Mr. Romano says if it happens again, the third time won't be the charm because he'll put me in detention."

"We're heading to art across the hall so we'll go with Valentina," adds Chloe, linking arms with Mariama.

"See you guys later," I answer. "I need to grab a folder from my locker."

My homeroom is just a few feet from my locker, so I don't have far to walk.

"How's it going, Sophie?" Nathan Jones, a boy I became friends with last year after we stood up to the class bully, catches up with me right after I slam my locker shut and start making my way to homeroom. "Anything interesting happen this weekend?"

"Nothing much, just the usual," I answer. "What about you?"

Nathan's pushes his sliding glasses up on the bridge of his nose. "Well, things have been busy at Fun Plex because there have been lots of end of the year parties, and my mom and I went to the post office to pick up and mail off some packages…"

The second bell rings.

"I'd better get into class, Nathan." I cut him off and rush to the doorway of my classroom. "If Mr. Romano sees me out of my seat when the final bell rings, I'm in for it. Maybe I'll see you at lunch."

He looks disappointed that we have to end our conversation, which is odd since we're friends but not besties or anything. I breathe a sigh of relief as I slide into my desk two seconds shy of the final bell.

Whew! That was close.

Chapter 3

The Gingerbread House

Another package is waiting for me when I get home.

"It's a gingerbread house kit!" I exclaim after I open the box. I read the typed letter that's tucked inside the bottom.

> *Dear Sophie,*
>
> *Have fun making and eating this "home sweet home."*
>
> *Your Secret Santa*

"This will be a fun activity for you kids to do with Granny Washington when she gets here tonight, says Mom. "I need to bake some cookies for Cole's class party, so she can keep you two occupied and out of the batter while I'm working."

"Your Secret Santa must want you guys to visit my office sooner than your next checkup," jokes my father after he walks in and we show him the newest gift. "You've been eating more than your share of sweets lately."

My father is a dentist with his own office in Houston, and my mother works with him, keeping the records and helping schedule patients. Since my parents see so many people with tooth problems, they limit how much candy Cole and I eat, and they pile on the veggies at meals. My dad eats so many salads that his teeth were tinted green at his last dental checkup.

My grandmother arrives at our house around 6:30 p.m. and Cole and I can't wait to get started on the gingerbread houses.

"Yay! Granny is here!" Cole whoops, giving her a hug that nearly knocks her over. Our dog Bertram starts getting excited too, and begins to yip and bark.

"Whoa, whoa, whoa!" says Dad, holding his arms out to calm us down as we jump up and down. "Let your grandma get herself settled."

"And I'm sure she needs to get something to eat before starting on that gingerbread house," scolds Mom.

"That's fine," says Granny, smiling. "I ate a chicken sandwich on the road. Let me put my bag in my room and freshen up for a minute and we can get started."

Granny lives in Corpus Christi, which is about a three-hour drive from our house in Houston. She comes to visit us three or four times a year and we always have lots of fun with her. Every summer we stay with her for a week at her house and have a blast playing on the beach and swimming in the Gulf of Mexico each day. When she comes to our house, she brings us neat gifts and makes us all our favorite things to eat.

"Wash your hands and clear the placemats off the table so you can get started when Granny comes out," instructs Mom.

Inside the box are gingerbread pieces shaped as the roof and sides of the gingerbread house, frosting to hold the sides together, and peppermints, and gumdrops to decorate the house with.

"Okay, let's make sure we get this straight," Grandma peers at the instruction sheet through her glasses.

Don't eat all the candy!" I fuss at Cole as he sneaks a gumdrop.

Then I slide a red gumdrop from my palm into my mouth to sample. *Not bad, I wonder whether the green one is lime or peppermint-flavored?*

Mmmmm, Mmmmm, Mmmm…Bertram starts begging once he sees my jaws moving.

"Just glop a little frosting on to hold the side up," suggests Cole, as he watches our grandmother trying to line the edges of the gingerbread house up perfectly.

She sighs as the piece for the roof falls off for the fourth time.

"We want it to look like the picture on the box," she says.

"Check in the pantry and see if there is any more frosting," grandma instructs, ignoring my comment.

"I have some extra that I'm not using with the cookies," offers Mom.

Cole gets it, and Granny Washington furrows her brow and keeps a steady hand as she uses the frosting to line the flat cookie up just right on the candy rooftop.

"Let's get back now," she shoos away Bertram who is still underfoot.

This is a side to my grandmother that I have never seen. When she takes over a project, Granny Washington means business. Dad once told us that his mother always kept things in order when he was growing up, but she usually plays with me and Cole and lets us make all kinds of messes during her visits.

My mother pulls three or four dozen cookies out of the oven, and we still haven't finished the gingerbread house.

"Can't we eat any of it yet, Granny?" Cole starts to whine.

"You all can put the gumdrops on," she lays the picture of the completed house on the table. We try to follow the pattern that is shown. Cole puts more gumdrops on one side of the roof than the other, and it starts to lean.

Grandma is getting more and more frustrated.

"Here, let me fix this," she says, adding more frosting to even things up.

"I'm going upstairs to take my bath," says Cole.

Granny Washington and I work hard the entire 40 minutes he is gone.

By nine o' clock, our gingerbread house looks just like the one on the box.

"Wow! That's great!" Mom exclaims. "Let me get my phone out to take a picture."

"Is the house ready to eat now?" Cole bounds in the rooms with a panting Bertram right behind him.

"Slow down, Son," warns Dad, "You're going to…"

"Cole, stop!" I yell.

"Uhhh ohhh!" My brother starts sliding in his feet pajamas and bumps into the kitchen table.

"Noooo!" I yell.

Things appear in slow motion as the gingerbread house shifts to the edge of the table, then stops.

It's still standing tall.

We all breathe a sigh of relief.

Suddenly, Bertram jumps up and chomps off half the roof.

Woof!

"Oh no!" Granny Washington exclaims.

Cole swipes a fallen chunk of gingerbread from the table, starts chewing, and grins.

"Mmmm, this is delicious, Grandma."

Granny just shakes her head.

"It's the perfect example of 'home *sweet* home," laughs my father, helping clean up the mess.

"Maybe we can get some individual ginger-bread men that each person can decorate on their own, tomorrow," says Mom, patting my grandmother on the back to console her.

Bertram looks up with a mouth covered with white frosting as if to smile.

Ruff!

Chapter 4

Ice Capades

Saturday morning, Chloe texts before I put my feet in my fuzzy, bunny slippers, inviting me to go ice skating at a rink near the mall.

[My mom can pick u up @2] says the message.

That sounds like fun, but I'm a little nervous. I've never been ice skating before, and the couple of times I've gone roller skating when I was smaller, I spent most of the afternoon holding my father's hand.

After I ask Mom at breakfast she gives Chloe's mother a call to make sure it's okay.

"You kids act like you are old enough to make plans for yourselves," she says shaking her head. Mom looks up the pricing for the skates on the rink's website and gives me money for entry and to rent skates.

"Chloe's mother says you will be skating for a couple hours. Here is some extra money for drinks and a snack," Mom says, "and take these mittens with you." She hands me a pair of purple hand coverings. "It might be cold in there."

I slip the mittens on my fingers to admire them. It usually doesn't get very cold here in Houston, so we don't use mittens or gloves much. I haven't had to wear a coat all week and it's December.

"Sophie gets to have all the fun!" pouts Cole, as I wait by the window for my friend to pick me up.

"Don't you worry about that, Cole," Dad pats his shoulders. "I'm heading to the gym to shoot some hoops this morning with the fellas. A couple of them are bringing their sons, so you can join us."

Cole perks up at that. "Yay! I can show my skills!"

My little brother loves basketball, and he's pretty good at it. Every fall he plays on a junior basketball league. This season, his coach moved him up to the point guard position because his shooting has really improved. Cole now says he wants to be an NBA player when he grows up, and he's been practicing his free throw shooting every afternoon. My father usually goes out to work with him when he gets home from his office, but Cole always likes to get extra playing time in with other kids.

The Thompson's arrive, and I am happy to see that my other friends, Mariama and Valentina, are also in the car. *This is going to be fun!*

"Long time, no see, Miss Sophie," says Chloe's mother. "You get prettier and more grown up every time I see you."

"Thank you, Mrs. Thompson," I say blushing.

It's crowded when we enter the ice skating rink, and popular music is blaring from the overhead speakers. The air is frosty, so I'm glad I'm wearing a jacket. Throngs of skaters expertly glide across the ice. A girl wearing a fancy ice skating outfit, who looks smaller than Cole, turns a perfect figure eight.

"I love this song," says Chloe excitedly. "Come on guys, let's get your skates."

She owns her own pair of skates, white with pink shoe laces, so I guess she knows what she's doing.

"I used to take ice skating lessons here," she explains when we admire how quickly she laces the boots on her feet.

"I can skate pretty well," says Valentina, handing over her shoes to the attendant as we get our rental skates. "I came to a *Frozen* birthday party here last year."

"This is my first time ice skating," says Mariama.

"I'm a newbie too," I chime in, gingerly moving on my blades toward the rink.

"Don't worry, guys, you'll catch on," soothes Chloe. Then she floats off on the ice graceful as a ballerina.

"Wait for us, Chloe!" Valentina wobbles a bit, but finds her footing, making her way toward our friend.

Mariama holds on the bars on the side of the rink and practices gliding.

"Here goes nothing," I say as I make my way to her side.

We wind around the circular rink once without falling, which is quite an accomplishment. I thought I would do better with ice skating since I went roller skating with my family when I was six or seven, but this is hard work. My ankles are aching from trying to keep my balance on the steel blades. *How do people stand doing this for hours?*

Chloe and Valentina have spun around the ice at least three times to our one, and now Chloe is skating backwards.

"Hey, isn't that Toby and Nathan?" Mariama points across the floor at two boys standing near our two cheer mates.

I squint to see. "Yeah, that's them," I answer. It's really surprising that they are together. Toby always teases Nathan because he is kind of awkward at sports, and just a few months ago Nathan was on the verge of dumping a bowl of salsa on Toby's head when they got into an argument during one of our school field trips.

Valentina whizzes up to us. "Look who Chloe invited to skate," she smiles. "Tus amantes, Sophie!"

"I don't even want to know what that means," I say, frowning at Valentina. Her family speaks Spanish at home and sometimes she uses it with us.

"It means that Nathan and Toby both like you," she answers. "and Chloe invited them here to find out which one is your secret Santa."

"You guys are crazy!" I say trying to move off the ice and onto the safety of the stable carpeted area. "neither one of them is my secret Santa!"

An upbeat hip hop song starts playing and the crowd begins to move faster. I teeter, and a little kid with neon green and orange colored earmuffs rams into my leg.

"Sorry," he says, as I slide to my knees. I wish I could disappear under the rink, as I shiver and use my hands to try to get back on my feet. It's freezing this close to the ice; I'm so happy that my mom gave me mittens to wear.

I see Nathan and Toby pointing from across the rink. Toby has his hand over his mouth to hide his laughter. Valentina whips out her cell phone and takes a picture.

Just great, I look like a fool in front of my potential secret Santas and maybe the world if Valentina posts this on Instapic.

"Are you all right, Sophie?" Nathan races over to help me to my feet.

"Thanks, Nathan, I'm fine," I say. "How'd you learn to skate so well?"

"We come here a lot in the summer," he answers. "My mom says it's a good place to beat the Texas heat."

Nathan helps me to the carpeted area and waits with me. A remake of the song, "Santa Claus is Coming to Town," starts to play.

"Christmas is one of my favorite times of year," I say.

"Yeah, I like getting gifts and getting a nice break from school," says Nathan.

"Speaking of gifts…" I begin.

Suddenly, Mariama plops down on the bench beside us. "Whew! I'm glad you're okay after that fall," she says. "Let's buy a snack."

"Yeah, I am getting hungry," answers Nathan.

After purchasing chips and bottled lemonade, we sit and watch the skaters for a while. The music slows down and Toby and Chloe make their way around the rink, deep in conversation. Valentina skates ahead of them and mouths the words to the song that's playing. Toby hasn't come over to speak and barely seems to notice the rest of us are here, so I doubt that he is my secret Santa.

Nathan, on the other hand, may be another story.

"I'm glad Chloe invited us to join you all here," he says. "My dad was going to make me go in to Fun Plex with him before she called."

Images of Nathan's father yelling at him behind the Fun Plex service desk float through my mind. Fun Plex is an entertainment center with bumper cars and video games that is a blast for most kids but that Nathan hates. His family bought the center a few years ago and he has to spend nearly every weekend and even some school holidays there helping out. Nathan's dad is pretty strict with him and gets really upset if he so much as drops a napkin. Before seeing 'Mean Mr. Jones' in action, I thought it would be cool to own a play place like Fun Plex, but afterwards I felt sorry for Nathan.

We rest on the benches for a few minutes with our soft drinks, and then Nathan guides me and Mariama back out onto the ice and helps us make our way around again. By the time we leave the rink two hours later, I feel like I've gotten the hang of ice skating.

"Thanks so much for skating with us, Nathan," I say as we wait for our parents to pick us up.

"Thank you all for inviting me," he says looking at Chloe. "This was fun."

"Yeah, I had a good time too," says Toby smiling. "There's my ride, see you all at school on Monday."

"See you!" we all chime as Mrs. Thompson pulls up, and Nathan also heads to his parents' white SUV.

Thankfully, Chloe's mother is on her cell phone so she isn't paying attention to the details of our conversation.

"You skated two hours and still didn't ask him if he is your secret Santa?" Chloe scolds me, when she learns I didn't find out if Nathan is sending the packages.

"It never seemed like the right time," I respond, realizing she is right.

"Well, at least we figured out who isn't her Santa," says Valentina. "You and Toby were making googly eyes at each other the entire time we were there."

Chloe just blushes because she knows it's true. If her mother wasn't in the car to hear she might deny it, but I can tell she doesn't want to draw attention to herself.

I'm still in the dark about who my secret Santa is. Nathan didn't mention anything about packages, so maybe he isn't sending the gifts. But he sure was acting nice. Maybe he is...

Chapter 5

Hoop Dreams

There are no packages from my secret Santa when I get home from ice skating, but there is an envelope.

"No box? Ah, man!" Cole sighs in disappointment. He and Dad got back home just a few minutes before I returned, but my father had to drive in to his dental office to do an emergency filling for a patient who fell off his bike and chipped a front tooth.

"I'm just glad there weren't any more sweets delivered," says Mom. "You two still haven't finished all the candy from the first package you got, and Cole was hyper half the night after eating that gingerbread."

"I guess that's why you didn't get us individual gingerbread men the next day like you said you would," Cole counters.

"You got that right, buddy," Mom laughs.

I open the letter.

Hope your holiday season is extra nice, just like you! Enjoy some time out during your vacation. My treat!

Your Secret Santa

"It's a ten dollar gift card to Studio Cinema Movie House!" I exclaim. "I've been wanting to go there since it opened last fall."

"Yeah, Jake told me they have huge movie screens," says Cole. "And they bring your food to you at your seat after you press a buzzer."

"This secret Santa person has been spending quite a bit on you, Sophie," says Mom. "Now I'm getting curious as to who it is."

"Is there a return address?" asks Granny Washington.

"No, the three things I've gotten so far have just had my name and address on them," I respond.

"Tomorrow, I may ask the mail carrier if there is any way we can trace where these gifts are coming from," says Mom.

"I'm going to go shoot some hoops," says Cole.

"Again? All right, Lebron," I tease him.

"Come back in in about an hour because dinner will be ready," Mom says to Cole. "And make sure to shut the door behind you completely. You left it cracked yesterday and a lizard got in the house."

"I'm glad I didn't see that," I shiver.

"Yeah, you would have been screaming louder than the fans at a Houston Rockets basketball game," Cole laughs and heads on out.

I sit on a bar stool at the kitchen island. The snack I had at the skating rink is long gone, and my stomach starts to growl.

Smells of garlic, spices, and chicken broth fill the house. Granny Washington must be making her famous soup! Usually, I hate to eat any dish with vegetables in it, but Granny's soup is "the bomb.com." She mixes in all sorts of tasty spices in a broth along with cut carrots, peas, green beans, potatoes, corn, and turkey sausage. Sounds too healthy to be good, but I love it. Even Cole gets seconds, and he can't stand to eat anything green.

"How'd you learn to cook so well, Granny?" I ask as she stirs in the large pan.

"Well, back in my day we all had to work in the kitchen," she says. "From the time I was younger than Cole, I was chopping vegetables and helping my own mother make breakfast, lunch and dinner."

I can make scrambled eggs and brownies from a mix, but that's about it. I would love to be a great chef like Granny.

"Next time you cook something, can I help?" I ask.

"Most certainly, young lady," she smiles.

The back door opens, then slams shut. Cole is back already.

"That was a quick practice session," says Mom, looking up from the book she's reading in the family room. "I didn't expect you'd come inside for another hour or so."

"I got tired," he says. "Think I'll go to my room for a while before dinner." He turns his head away from us.

"Wait a minute," I say. "Why are there grass stains on the back of your shorts? I thought you were shooting baskets?"

"I don't know, I may have gotten them before I went to the gym with Dad," Cole replies breathlessly, moving toward the staircase. Then he bounds up the stairs.

Mom curls back up with her book and Grandma dumps cornmeal in a bowl to make corn muffins. They don't seem to notice anything, but this is strange. Cole NEVER willingly stops playing basketball. Mom has to scream at him to come in to eat almost every day. That novel she is reading for her book club must be really good because I can't believe she doesn't realize something is going on.

I tiptoe up the staircase to investigate. Cole's door is ajar, so I creep up and peek through the crack. He's not there. I open the door all the way and look in. Cole's bed is made more neatly than normal because Granny Washington probably came in to clean up after him. As usual, his Star Wars Jedi light saber, pirate suit, cowboy hat and other dress up gear are on his toy box, rather than inside it, where they belong. Nothing seems amiss.

I turn and head back down the hall toward my room and catch Cole shutting my parent's door.

"What's up?" I ask.

"Nothing," Cole answers, moving out of the light. He jerks his hand behind his back.

"Are you hiding something?" I reach out to grab his arm and my brother moves away from me.

"Leave me alone, Sophie!" he cries.

"Why are you coming out of Mom and Dad's room? What's in your hand? Let me see it," I demand.

Cole keeps pulling away.

"If you don't show me what that is, I'm telling," I threaten.

"Then I'll tell Mom that you forgot to feed Bertram last week!" he retorts.

"Too late, I already told her before school on Friday," I respond. Surprisingly, she wasn't mad. Probably because Cole feeds our dog so many extra treats on a regular day it didn't hurt him much to miss one meal.

Reluctantly, Cole opens his fist. Inside is a bottle of Mom's face makeup.

"What in the world are you doing with that?" I laugh. "Dressing up as Miss America?"

Cole moves closer to the light and I get a better view of his face. The skin around his eye is puffy and his nose is Rudolph red.

"Wow! What happened to you?"

Chapter 6

Christmas Decoration

"Looks like your face got decorated, just in time for Christmas!" I joke.

"Promise you won't tell Mom and Dad!" Cole demands, moving into the doorway of my room.

I follow him in and shut the door.

"Why should I promise you that?" I answer. "They'll just make you confess anyway."

"Please, Sophie! I don't want them to know!" he pleads.

His eyes start to water. Something serious must have gone down because, though he's only eight years old, Cole is pretty tough. He's the kind of kid who's the first one to jump in the deep end before he can swim.

"All right, all right, I won't tell," I promise. "Now what happened?"

"I got into a fight," he answers, "with Rhythm Brown."

"That new kid who lives down the street?" I ask.

The Brown family moved to our subdivision from another area of Houston about four months ago. Rhythm is Cole's age but acts like he's older than me sometimes. His parents are divorced; his mother lets him go to PG-13 movies and he doesn't even have a bedtime.

"Yeah, Rhythm and his little brother Blu keep messing with me every time I go out to practice," says Cole. "Today I got tired of it and shoved him, then Blu held me Rhythm hit me in the nose."

Thank goodness it didn't start bleeding. I feel like hurting those jerks.

"Why are they messing with you, Cole?" I ask. "What are they saying?"

"They keep making fun of how I dress and calling me 'bougie boy' because we are in private school and don't take the bus with everyone else."

We have to wear a uniform every day at Xavier Academy, the private school we've attended since preschool: khakis and polo shirts for boys, and khakis, or skirts, and polos for girls. When it comes to following the dress code rules, our teachers don't play. Your shirt better be tucked in, and you'd better wear a belt with your slacks or you will be sent straight to the principal's office for detention.

"That is so silly, Cole," I say, shaking my head. "You should ignore them when they come around and not bother with them."

"Believe me, I've tried that," he argues. "They keep coming up and pushing me around. After he hit me, Rhythm said he better not see me outside."

This is more serious than I thought. Something will have to be done.

"Cole! Sophie! Time for dinner!" Mom calls.

"Quick, let's try to cover up your eye before we go downstairs," I say. "You don't want Mom, Dad or Granny to ask any questions."

I pour a little bit of my mother's makeup in my palm and dab it around Cole's eye like I see her pat it on her skin when she's going out on dates with Dad.

"Here, let me smooth it in a little more," I instruct before releasing him to make his way downstairs to dinner.

Not bad. I think once we get to the table. *I could get a job at the makeup counter at the mall.*

Dad is back from taking care of his patient and lectures us about what happened.

"Make sure you kids wear your helmets whenever you ride your bikes," he warns. "The boy I was working on almost lost his permanent front tooth after his fall, luckily we were able to save it."

"Listen to your father, kids. Things are just so dangerous now," agrees Granny Washington. "They aren't making these bicycles as sturdy as they used to."

It's been at least ten minutes, and no one has noticed anything amiss about Cole's swollen eye. It helps that his caramel complexion perfectly matches Mom's. We finish dinner and Granny insists on cleaning the dishes so Cole and I get out of doing our regular chores.

"Come to my room before you go downstairs in the morning so I can put on your makeup," I whisper to my brother as we get turn to go upstairs after watching *How the Grinch Stole Christmas* and *Frosty the Snowman Christmas* specials.

"Seeing those old shows really gets me in the holiday spirit," says Grandma. "We need to decorate for Christmas around here soon."

"Yeah, I think I will put the lights up tomorrow afternoon," says my father. "Maybe we can go buy a tree after church."

"I want a big one this season," says my mother. "Not like that Charlie Brown Christmas-sized one we got last year."

I giggle to myself as I think how, unbeknownst to them, the holiday decorations have already started, with my little brother's face.

"Goodnight, Mom and Dad. Goodnight, Granny Washington," I say. "See you in the morning, Cole."

Chapter 7

Deck the Halls

Sunday is a no-mail day, so I'm disappointment when I realize I won't be getting a gift from my secret Santa. It's been just three days, but I've already gotten used to hearing from him each afternoon. I wonder if anyone buys my Santa gifts or if he wishes I could send him something. I would if he left a return address. It's nice being thought of by someone special.

After church, Cole and I change into our play clothes and head outside to watch Dad put up the Christmas lights. The swelling around my brother's eye went down last night, and it wasn't too red this morning so I didn't have to put much make up on to mask where he got hit.

Though it's bright and sunny outside and nearly seventy-five degrees, it truly seems like holiday time because many of neighbors already have lights, wreaths and holiday inflatables and figurines out.

"Hand me that white extension cord, Sophie," my father calls from the ladder he is standing on to string lights around the roof. My mother gets nervous every year when he does this and tells him he should hire a company to put up the lights.

"Decorating our house is part of the fun of the holiday season," he always answers, "and I want to do it myself."

For the next hour, Dad strings up red, green, yellow, and blue lights around the front of the roof top. He puts light up reindeer and a metal Bumble the abominable snowman in the yard. I can't wait to see the glowing decorations when the sun goes down.

Inside the house, Granny and my mother play holiday music.

"Come in and help us get the garland up," Mom calls from the door, over the sound of "All I Want for Christmas is You," playing.

My father has finished up outside and drives to a nearby garden center to get our Christmas tree.

While my mother and I twine garland around the staircase banisters near our formal living room, Granny Washington and Cole search for our box of Christmas ornaments, so we'll be ready when the tree gets here.

"Not bad," my mother gives her seal of ap-proval after Dad brings in a fluffy, six-foot, pine tree. Our house fills with the woodsy, fresh, evergreen scent.

"Now it feels like the holidays!" Granny Washington smiles.

Cole cracks a corny joke. "What do you get if you cross an apple with a Christmas tree? A pineapple!"

Dad untangles and drapes the lights on the tree, then we have fun putting up the ornaments. My mother buys Cole and me new ones each year that reflect the activities we are in. Last year, when I won the spelling bee, she bought me a blue ribbon ornament. Cole's art was featured in the Houston Livestock and Rodeo youth contest, so he got an ornament shaped like a paintbrush. My new ornament for this season is a cheerleading megaphone with my name and the year on it, and Cole has a mini basketball. Mom also bought Bertram an ornament shaped like a man's dress shoe since he loves chewing up Dad's loafers so much.

"Thanks, Mom!" I exclaim, giving her a hug. "These are so cute."

"What thoughtful mementos," Granny Washington says. She gives us hooks to hang them on the tree.

Once all the ornaments are in place, Dad boosts up Cole to place the star on top. We drink hot apple cider and hot chocolate to celebrate after we are done.

"Deck the halls with boughs of holly, fa la la la la, la la la laaaaah!" sings Cole.

Chapter 8

Rhythm is Gonna Getcha

By Monday morning, the swelling on Cole's face has gone down completely so there is no need to put any more of Mom's makeup on him. I sneak the bottle of foundation back into the master bathroom before breakfast.

On our drive to school, I glance over at the bus stop to see if I spot Rhythm. I had never paid much attention to him before because he is just a little kid like Cole, but I can see how he might scare my brother.

Rhythm's hair is dyed blond on the tips and styled in a faded cut on the side with lines in it, and he wears his loose jeans in a saggy style my parents hate, topped by a ripped, red and black leather jacket. His neon green and turquoise high-top tennis shoes are an expensive brand that my parents won't buy for Cole.

At first, Cole is too busy reading his chapter book from English class to notice, but both Rhythm and seven-year-old Blu mean mug our car as we drive by. Cole looks out the window, and Rhythm, who is several inches taller than Cole, makes a fist and starts punching it in his palm. Blu is big for his age too, and looks more like Rhythm's twin than his little brother.

Cole's eyes get wide and he quickly turns away. He squints to keep from crying.

Why do they hate my brother so much? He's a super nice kid and pretty funny if you like corny jokes. Must be jealous, I figure.

Cole is always outside playing basketball with our father, and once when we rode our bikes by their house, I heard Rhythm and Blu's mother fuss at their dad about how he never comes to see the kids. Ms. Brown is from Vietnam, and their father grew up here in Houston and is a drummer in a jazz band. He travels around the world playing music and is hardly ever around.

Cole gets on my nerves sometimes, and I pick on him myself, but as Granny Washington says, "Blood is thicker than water." Those bullies aren't going to rough up my little brother and get away with it.

"See you later, Mom, love you!" I say as Cole and I hop out of the car near the school entrance.

"See you, kids. Good luck on your English quiz, Cole!" she calls.

As soon as Mom drives out of the car pool line, I pull Cole aside.

"Don't worry about Rhythm and Blu, little brother. I will come up with a way to deal with them. I don't want you to be scared playing in our neighborhood again, okay?"

"But what will you do, Sophie?" he asks, eyes wide. "I don't want you to get into any trouble."

"I'm not sure yet, Squirt, but I'll figure something out." I give Cole a quick hug and pat him on the back before he skip-steps toward the lower school and I rush to the area for middle school students.

A sweet, cinnamon scent wafts through the air as I approach my locker. My friends Valentina and Mariama are standing nearby. Chloe has a field trip with her English class today to see the Nutcracker ballet, so we probably won't see her until tomorrow.

Yay! Valentina has brought in churros again. Her grandmother, or abuela as she calls her, is just as great a cook as Granny Washington. At least once every couple of weeks Mrs. Martinez sends in yummy snacks for us to share.

"Buenos dias, Sophie!" Valentina smiles, holding out the tasty bag of pastry treats, miraculously still warm. "Que pasa?"

I've been around Valentina so long that I know that she's saying, "Good morning, what's up?"

I just know I'll get an 'A' in Spanish class when we have to take it next year because I've learned hundreds of Spanish words during our conversations.

"I'm trying to figure out what to do about a boy from my neighborhood who is bullying Cole," I answer between nibbles. "You know that boy Rhythm I showed you from down the street? He hit Cole and has him scared to go outside."

"That's just terrible!" Mariama exclaims. "Poor little Cole!"

"Good morning, ladies." Toby Johnson ambles up with his hands out for a churro. Normally, he doesn't bother to spend time with us at our lockers unless Chloe is around, preferring to play with the other boys in the gym, but he likes good food better than early morning basketball.

"The price for a churro is the magic word," says Valentina, pulling the bag behind her back.

"Pleeeease?" he coos, flashing his straight white teeth and showing his dimple.

I can't help but smile. When he first moved to Texas from Ohio, I had a serious crush on Toby. I even pretended I love to watch basketball, which I can't stand unless Cole is playing, to get his attention. I still like Toby a little bit, but I wouldn't admit it to anyone. He's sweet on Chloe, and she doesn't seem to mind when he comes around like she did when he first transferred to Xavier. Everyone in our grade calls them ToChlo behind their backs.

"Sophie was just telling us about some boy named Rhythm who is being mean to her little brother," blabs Valentina. "We need to find out a way to stop it."

"Cole's a cool dude," says Toby. "We can't have that. I'll definitely help. I know that Rhythm kid, he's annoying. He was teasing my little brother Michael a few months back, and we did something to shut him down, really quick. Don't worry, Sophie," Toby puts his arm around my shoulder. "I'll put Rhythm in his place by tomorrow."

"What are you going to do, Toby?" I ask worriedly. "I don't want to hurt him or anything, and what if a teacher or our parents find out?"

"Don't worry," he winks. "It will be our secret."

Chapter 9

Bus Stop

I don't think too much about my conversation with Toby during the school day, but on our way home as we pass the area of the neighborhood school bus stop, I start getting nervous about it again. The last thing I want to do is start a fight with anyone. In fifth grade, a girl named Lanie Mitchell was bullying me and my friends, and things got so bad that Nathan Jones ended up in the hospital with a busted leg. Lanie got kicked out of Xavier after I told the principal what she was doing. I learned then that the best way to deal with bullies was to let grownups know what's going on. If Toby's solution with Rhythm doesn't work, I will have to break my promise to Cole and tell Mom and Dad because I know first hand what can happen if things go too far.

After we finish our snack, I hear my cell phone vibrate and check it. It's a message from Toby! [Meet me in your driveway at 4. Bring Cole]

[K, C U] I respond.

It's on now! I wonder what Toby has up his sleeve.

"We've got to go out to the driveway at four o' clock," I whisper to my brother.

"What for?" he answers, looking scared.

"Remember my friend Toby who transferred to my class? He's going to help us with our neighbors," I answer.

Cole shakes his head in agreement and gets busy with his math homework.

Around three forty-five I slide my chair away from the kitchen table and pick up Bertram's leash.

"Mom, Granny, Cole and I are taking the dog for a walk," I say.

"Okay, sweetie." Mom barely glances up from some bills she's paying.

My grandmother just mumbles, she's so interested in the television soap opera she's watching.

"That Julia knows she likes some Victor!" Granny cries out as if I know what is happening on the television love triangle.

"Come on, Cole, let's go." I grab him by the hand.

Rhythm and Blu have really got my brother shaken because he's moving slower than a snail as we go through the garage to the driveway.

Bertram is excited to be getting out and tugs on his leash.

Woof! Woof! Our dog barks as he spots Toby and his younger brother Michael moving our way down the street.

My classmate doesn't seem to have a care in world as he whistles up to our driveway in sweatpants and sneakers, dribbling a basketball. He grins widely as Cole and I move toward our basketball goal.

"Great, you made it right on time," he praises Cole and me, and pats Bertram's head. "The school bus should get getting here any minute."

I forgot that other schools in our district don't release at 3 p.m. like Xavier, and that Rhythm, Blu and the other kids from our neighborhood come home around this time.

"What are we going to do when they get off the bus, Toby?" Cole starts shaking.

"Let me handle it, little man," Toby replies. "Why don't you and Michael play a game of Knockout while we wait?"

Cole is happy to have a partner to play with and quickly bounces his basketball to the goal. He and Michael aren't close friends since they are not in the same class at school, but Cole has played against him in the junior basketball league once and is always up for competition.

While we are standing on the curb, the mail truck pulls up. Bertram barks again, annoyed that we aren't going on a walk after all. I let go of his leash so he can run around the yard.

"Another delivery for Sophie Washington," says the mail carrier, handing me a new secret Santa box.

"Thanks," I say taking it and running the package up to the front door.

"You get lots of mail?" asks Toby. "Must be nice."

"I have been getting packages every day since last week," I answer. "I'm not sure where they are coming from."

"I like to mail things," Toby replies, and I raise my eyebrow. *Maybe he is my Santa!*

"Here they come!" interrupts Cole, stopping his game with Michael.

While Toby and I were talking, the yellow school bus stopped and dropped off kids.

Rhythm and Blu stomp straight to our driveway and corner Cole, not noticing Toby and me by the mailbox.

"Hey, 'Bougie boy,' what's up? Want some more of what we gave you on Saturday?"

"What did you give him?" Toby walks up and joins the conversation. "Maybe I can return the favor."

"You too weak to stand up to me yourself, 'Bougie boy?'" taunts Rhythm. "Have to bring your big sissy and her friends to help you out?"

Bertram senses something is wrong and starts growling.

"Cole doesn't have to stand up to anybody," Toby answers. "He's in his own yard, minding his own business, something that you and your little brother here need to do too."

"And if we don't, what are you going to do about it?" sneers Blu. "Me and my brother are both black belts in Tae Kwan Do, and we can beat all of you and your dirty dog too."

Bertram growls again.

"Oh, we're not going to fight you," says Toby smiling. "We're just going to spread Rhythm's little secret."

Chapter 10

The Pull Up

Rhythm narrows his eyes. "You don't know any secret about me."

"Oh, yes we do," answers Michael. "Didn't you go to the Rockets basketball day camp?" he asks.

"Yeah, Michael told us the funniest story that week," recalls Toby. "About a boy with a weird name that started with an 'R' who was crying when his father dropped him off and who wet his pants on the first day of camp.

"The camp counselors didn't have any clean underwear to put on him until his mother could come to get him, so he had to wear a giant pull up," Michael laughs, "and 'Pull up' was the nickname the big boys called him for the rest of the week."

"That was a while ago," Rhythm says, lip trembling.

"It was this past fall break." Toby moves closer to him. "And if you don't leave my friend here alone, I'll make sure that everybody in the neighborhood knows about it."

Rhythm backs off and starts moving down the street. "Come on, Blu, we don't need to waste time with these liars, let's go home."

Ruff! Ruff! Bertram angrily barks at the boys and they back off down the driveway.

"Thanks so much, Toby!" I smile as the brothers disappear down the block.

"Yeah, thanks!" Cole smiles widely.

"No problem, anything for a friend," he grins. "That should take care of those two, but if they try anything else, just let me know."

We play Knockout on the basketball goal for the next hour. I'm terrible at sports and miss all but one of my shots, but it's fun spending time with Toby.

"Follow through with your wrists after you release the ball," he advises.

The game stops when Mom calls Cole and me in to get cleaned up for dinner.

"We need to head home too," Toby says. "See you at school tomorrow, Sophie."

"See you!" I respond.

There was so much excitement that I almost forget my package. I open the front door and grab it on my way to my room.

"What did you get this time?" Cole peers over my shoulders.

"Scented pencils!" I exclaim, ripping the brown paper off the box.

"Another gift from this Santa person," says Mom. "I forgot to try to find out who it is."

"If they were colored pencils I could use them for my drawings," says Cole, losing interest. Cole is very talented in art and has won painting and drawing contests at our school and at the Houston Rodeo last year.

"Well they are for me, not you, and I think they are cool," I answer, sniffing a lemon-scented pencil.

Like my other gifts, this one has a letter from my secret Santa.

> *Hope these pencils make studying your spelling words sweet!*
>
> *Your Secret Santa*

I'm happy my secret Santa thinks about me every day. I am getting more and more curious about who is giving me these presents. I remember how Toby said he likes to mail things right before we went to save Cole from Rhythm and Blu. Could he be my Santa?

Chapter 11

Mystery Man

"My bet is still on Nathan Jones," says Mariama after I tell her about yesterday's showdown with Rhythm and Blu, my recent secret Santa gift, and my new suspicions about Toby, as we stand at our lockers. "Toby sweet talks everybody."

She points across the hallway and, sure enough, Toby is laughing with Carly Gibson and her twin brother Carlton. He pats Carly on the arm and smiles.

Chloe glances their way and looks a teensy bit jealous. "Toby is kind of sometimey," she says, twirling one of her thick black curls with her finger. "Who knows? Maybe your Santa is someone you never met."

"But is seems like this person knows me somehow," I answer. "The first gift was all my favorite candies, even black licorice. How would anyone know that?"

"You've got a point," Chloe answers, scrunching up her nose. "I don't know too many people who want black licorice. I prefer red Twizzlers myself."

"And yesterday's note said something about my studying spelling words. I won the spelling bee last year, so it has to be someone who knows things about me."

"Those are all good points, Sophie," says Mariama. "We need to investigate to get to the bottom of this."

"But how?" Chloe answers.

"Sophie's going to have to get over her shyness and just ask those boys if they are her Santa," says Valentina.

"I guess, so…" I answer. "But if I spoil the surprise, I may stop getting gifts."

"Maybe you should try to figure it out on your own until Christmas break," suggests Chloe. "Then ask this Friday before we are off school if you can't figure it out. That way, if they stop giving you gifts you will get your real Santa gifts on Christmas Day a few days later."

"Good idea!" I exclaim.

"I wish I could have been there when Toby put Rhythm in his place," giggles Valentina, changing the subject. "That would have been a great photo for Instapic!"

Valentina loves to take photos with her cell phone and post them on social media sites, sometimes at the most inconvenient times. I'm lucky she didn't put the pictures from when I fell at the skating rink online.

"A better picture would be Rhythm wearing his saggy jeans with pull ups!" I laugh.

Nathan Jones stops by our locker on his way down the hall. "Hi, girls, what did you think about our science homework last night?"

Though I beat him in the spelling bee last year, Nathan is one of the smartest kids in our grade, and he loves science. He's been doing some special experiment with a frog for the past few months that he plans to enter in the science fair.

"I'm glad we won't have our test on the periodic table until after the holidays," I answer. "Because it is getting harder for me to focus."

"I'm not gonna lie, I didn't even get to it," admits Valentina. "We only get a participation grade for it don't we? Mi abuela made some delicioso cookies and we spent the evening eating and listening to Christmas music after dinner. I'm just ready for break to be here."

"Nice bracelet, Nathan," Chloe says as she admires a braided red, green, and yellow piece of jewelry on his wrist.

"Thanks, I got it yesterday as an early holiday gift," he answers, looking funny at the three of us. "Do you like it?"

"It's like those cute loom bracelets you used to make last year, Sophie," Mariama says.

"You know how to make these?" Nathan looks at me. "Say, Sophie…"

The first warning bell rings, and Valentina scoops up her backpack and starts moving down the hallway.

"See you guys at lunch," she says, changing the subject. "I'm glad we only have a few more days of school before Christmas break, so we won't have to rush to class or worry about yucky science."

"Yeah, it will be nice to have a break from all the school work," I agree. "See you later!"

I grab my messenger bag and move the other way toward my homeroom. Nathan holds his hand up as if to stop me and then changes his mind and goes in the other direction.

Once again, I slide into my homeroom seat just in time to avoid being marked tardy. I wonder why Nathan keeps coming by my locker so often? He's been acting funny, like wants to tell me something. Could Nathan be the mystery man?

Chapter 12

Snow Day

It seems colder outside as I get in the Mom's car at pickup. I'm glad I wore my coat to school. Time flies by as I tune out Cole's chatter on the homeward ride. I'm excited to find out if I got another package.

Just as I expected, there's another box waiting for me on the kitchen counter and today's secret Santa gift is the best one yet!

"I love it!" I say, opening a heart-shaped locket with room for a picture inside.

"Your Santa has to be a girl," says Cole, frowning at the small piece of silver. "What boy would want to buy jewelry?"

"Is there a note? What does it say?" asks my mother, looking closer at the box.

> *Hope your day is filled with friendship and sunshine!*
>
> *Your Secret Santa*

"I wonder where all these presents are coming from?" ponders Granny Washington. "It is odd that no one has come forward."

"Look, there is a delivery address on the top of the box under the brown wrapping paper!" my mother exclaims. "It says Westmeyer Girls' Center. That's the foster home for girls on the other side of town. Who would be sending Sophie a gift from there?"

Her cell phone rings, and Mom stops talking to take the call.

"What? Are you sure? I can't believe it!"

She turns to us. "Turn on the television to channel fifteen, kids. Your dad just called with some exciting news!"

"An unexpected snowstorm is moving though the area," says the newscaster. "We predict from two to three inches of snow by tomorrow morning. All Houston area schools will be closed."

"Yay!" My brother and I give each other a high-five.

"Maybe we won't have to go back to school until after Christmas break," I say.

"Never in a million years would I expect it to snow here in Houston at Christmastime," smiles Mom. "But I did notice the temperature was unusually cool when I picked you up this afternoon."

"Do you want to build a snowman?" Cole sings the song from the movie *Frozen*. I groan and Granny Washington and my mother laugh.

"We haven't had snow in Houston in eight years," Mom declares. "Your father seems as excited as you kids."

"He probably is thrilled," says Granny Washington. "We never got snow when he was a boy in Corpus Christi."

Around five o'clock, the snow begins to fall. It's neat watching the flakes blanket the ground. Usually, it's warm in Houston. Last Christmas, some of our neighbors went swimming in their backyard pool, so this is a real treat.

"Let's go outside!" shouts Cole. "I want to touch fresh powder."

"Make sure you wear your coats and gloves," Mom warns. "And put these hats on too. You're not used to cold weather and you might get sick."

We wrap up as quickly as possible and run out in the front yard with our dog behind us. Bertram barks and jumps, trying to catch snowflakes. Cole twirls around alongside him.

Within fifteen minutes, there is enough snow on the ground to make actual snowballs. I am grateful that Mom made us bundle up. I thought snow would feel soft and cottony like it looks on television, but packed into balls, it is hard and freezing cold.

"Let's build snow angels!" I call.

Suddenly, something whacks me on the side of my head.

"Why'd you do that, Cole?!!!" I cry angrily, rubbing my scalp. Another ice ball flies through the air and scrapes my cheek.

"Ouch!" I scream.

I whirl around to confront my brother, but he seems as confused as I am.

"It's coming from over there!" He points to a bush at the end of the driveway.

A huge wad of snow hurls toward Bertram.

Woof! Woof! He shifts from playmate to guard dog and bounds down the driveway to investigate.

A dark tuft of hair with blond tips jerks down beneath the greenery.

"It's Rhythm!" I cry. "Get him, Bertram!"

Grrrrr! growls our dog chasing our neighbor around the bush.

"Get him away!" Rhythm calls. "That thing is going to bite me."

"Mamma!" Blu runs out from behind his brother.

Bertram's black fur stands on end, and he bares his teeth.

"You need to get out of our yard and leave me and my brother alone!" I shout. "We're tired of your bullying."

"Sophie Washington! What is going on here?" My mother peeks her head out of the side door. "I know I didn't hear you order Bertram to attack another child!"

Rhythm and Blu use the distraction to slide off down the ice-covered street, and my mother calls us inside.

"They've been messing with Cole whenever he goes outside to play," I protest, "and Rhythm was hitting us with snowballs when we were outside."

"That's still no reason for you children to sic our dog on people. One of you could have been hurt or Bertram could be taken in by the pound for being aggressive," Mom says. "I know you are excited with the snow, but I expect you to use better sense. Now come in and sit down somewhere."

I go to the couch and pout and Cole draws pictures of snowmen on a piece of paper. I don't see why my mother doesn't take our side. Usually, she fusses at me for being mean to my brother and now that I'm standing up for him she's mad. The snow has stopped falling, but a thick coating covers the lawn. You can't see the footprints from where Rhythm was running in our driveway anymore.

As soon as he steps in from the garage, our father wants to get out into the snow. "I may have to challenge you kids to a snowball fight," he teases.

"They've had their fill of hurling snow," says our mother. She tells him about the showdown with Rhythm and Blu.

"Your mother is right, kids," Dad says. "You shouldn't fight with our neighbors or have Bertram attacking them, but I am happy to see you standing up for your little brother, Sophie."

I smile. At least someone understands.

"Now let's go outside and have some fun before the snow melts!"

Mom gets on her coat too, and we pelt each other with clumps of snow. My mother and I are on a team against Dad and Cole.

"Gotcha!"

I whoop after I hurl a huge wad of snow at my brother. Mom hits Dad on the shoulder with another snowball, and some neighbors who are out building a snowman applaud.

"We're the winners!" I laugh as Granny Washington calls us in to get ready for dinner.

"I'm sorry for calling Bertram on our neighbors," I tell mom when we are on our way into the house.

"I know you were just trying to defend yourself, sweetie," Mom says, wrapping her arm around me.

I feel better about everything once we sit down to another one of Granny's delicious dinners of baked chicken, mashed potatoes, and roasted vegetables.

"Hold the broccoli," says Cole as he passes his plate to Granny to be served.

"Give him an extra helping," Dad interrupts and winks. "He might need it to give him strength for the next snowball showdown!"

Chapter 13

The Real Santa Claus

The snow and ice completely melt the day after the storm so, unfortunately, we have to go to school on Friday. The good news is that it's the last day before winter break.

"Hurry up, Cole!"

We are running late in the morning because my brother couldn't find his math notebook, so we have to rush through the front door of the school before the first warning bell rings. I zip around the corner of the hallway where my locker is and ram into Nathan Jones holding a box wrapped in brown paper. My backpack hits the floor, and Nathan's present goes flying across the hallway.

"Oops! Sorry!" I scramble to help him and then drop my backpack.

"Here, let me help you with that." Nathan reaches his free arm out and I use it to get my balance.

"I've been catching you when you fall a lot lately," he laughs as the second bell sounds.

"Hey, Jones, this present has your name on it," Toby says, tossing the box across the body-filled hallway.

"Thanks, man." Nathan grabs the gift and turns back to me. "Hey, Sophie, about this box…"

"Excuse me, but I really have to get to class," I interrupt and heft up my backpack. "I've been late too many times already, and there's no way I want to be in detention during winter break. See you at lunch?"

"Okay, sure, see you…" Nathan says. I'm halfway down the hall and make it in my seat right after the bell rings. Mr. Romano stares at me, raises his right eyebrow, shuts the door, and begins calling roll.

"I've got to start getting to homeroom earlier next year," I think as we listen to the principal give the morning announcements over the intercom. I'm glad Mr. Romano didn't call me out. Maybe he's feeling the holiday spirit.

The bell rings to signal the end of homeroom.

"Wait, Miss Washington, I need to give you something," the homeroom teacher calls out to me as everyone begins to file out the door for first period.

"Oooh, you're in for it!" Bentley Watson smirks as he heads out the door.

My stomach drops to my feet. *Please don't let this be a detention slip!*

"This was delivered to you from the front office this morning," Mr. Romano says holding out a box wrapped in familiar brown paper. Another secret Santa gift!

I hurry to my locker to sneak a peek before I have to get to my next class. It's an illustrated picture book of famous female African American leaders.

"This is really cute!" I say.

May all your dreams come true!

Your Secret Santa

I look around the hallway to see if any of my friends are around. Is Santa someone else in my class?

The rest of the morning stays hectic as my English, science, and math teachers give us pop quizzes to cram in last minute grades before the end of the term. You'd think they'd want to give us a little holiday treat before our break, but no such luck.

"What's up, Sophie?" greets Toby as I join our group at our usual table at lunch. "How was your day off?"

"We had lots of fun playing in the snow," I say. "My parents and Cole and I had a snowball fight."

"We made a huge snowman, taller than my brother Hector," says Valentina, pulling out her cell phone to show the photo of a five-foot snowman with a carrot nose and a Mexican-style sombrero hat on his head.

"My dad bought a sled so we could slide down that big hill in your subdivision, Sophie," says Mariama.

"Lucky!" I exclaim. "I've been down that hill. I'll bet that was fun!"

Since we rarely have real winter weather, our neighborhood association brings in snowmaking machines each January that creates artificial ice and snow for kids to slide on.

The boys settle down at the other end of the table, and Chloe pulls out a large pink tote bag.

"Since Christmas is in just a few days I brought you all your presents."

"You didn't have to get us gifts, Chloe," I say. I feel bad because I usually bring my friends presents during the holidays, but with all the excitement about trying to figure out who my Santa is, I didn't remember.

"Yeah, I totally forgot to get you guys gifts," says Mariama.

"Don't worry about that I just wanted to give these to you," Chloe replies, passing out small gold gift boxes to each of us.

We each take a peek.

"Thank you, Chloe! This is muy bonito!" says Valentina, so excited that she starts speaking Spanish as she admires the package of three mini bottles of red, white, and navy blue nail polish. We all got the same gift.

"They are our school colors so we can wear them when we cheer at our games," Chloe says.

"Cool idea!" Mariama agrees.

"Awesome! Presents!" calls Nathan Jones, walking toward our table with his lunch tray and seeing the gifts.

"Sorry, Nathan, these are for the girls," says Chloe, tossing her black curls. "I made some Christmas cookies to bring in for everyone the day before yesterday, but we ate them at home when we got snowed in."

"He's not missing out on presents," interrupts Toby, sliding back down to our end of the table. "I saw Nathan with a huge box this morning before school, right, Sophie? Or did Loverboy here bring that present for you?"

"Cut it, Toby," I say, blushing. "I have no idea what you are talking about. Nathan didn't bring me a gift."

"Yeah, he's such a goody, goody, try-hard, it was probably a giant apple for one of his teachers," Toby snickers.

"Not that it's any of your business, 'NBA All-Star wannabe,'" Nathan cuts in. "But the gift was a present someone sent me."

Toby steps up closer to him and raises to his full height, appearing even taller than Nathan than he already is.

I don't know why, but Toby and Nathan always seem to start fighting lately when our group is together. Toby makes fun of Nathan because he isn't the best at sports and spends a lot of time in the science lab, and Nathan acts like Toby isn't very smart. I'd better step in and put an end to this.

"Who'd you get the present from, Nathan?" I ask.

"My secret Santa," he says, looking at me questioningly.

"Sophie has been getting gifts from her secret Santa too!" Mariama barges in.

"Is this your first secret Santa present, Nathan?" adds Chloe, playing with the silver charm bracelet on her wrist.

"No, I've been getting them all week," he says, adjusting his glasses. "The latest one came from my homeroom teacher today. It was a science kit."

"I got a present in my homeroom today, too," I say, pulling the package out of the backpack.

"Has anyone been sending you anything, Toby?" Valentina asks him, and he shakes his head no.

"Any of you?" he replies.

"Nada," Valentina shakes her head.

"Well, I guess that rules the two boys out as your secret Santas, Sophie," Mariama says, breaking the baffled silence.

"I've been trying to ask if you were getting me these presents all week!" Nathan exclaims. He picks up the package I pulled out. "It looks like they are both coming from the same person because the brown wrapping paper and the writing on your box looks just like mine."

"There isn't a return address on any of the packages; they just have my name and notes wishing me good things." I pause. "But my mom found an address written on one of my packages that is from a girl's home across town."

"Wait a minute! I saw a crumpled flyer from that place in the bottom of one of my boxes, too," says Nathan. "Maybe our Santa lives there!"

"That sounds a little creepy," says Toby. "Why would someone in a girl's home be sending you two gifts?"

"I'm not sure, Toby," I say, "but I'm going to find out."

Chapter 14

The Other Side of Town

"Come on, guys, follow me," I take my lunch tray to the front of the cafeteria to dump my empty chocolate milk carton and other trash.

Then I walk next door to the school library, sit down at one of the computers and log on.

"What are you doing, Sophie?" asks Toby, leaning over my shoulder.

"I'm looking up the Westmeyer Girls' Center to see if I can guess who the secret Santa might be," I reply.

"Well, let me know what you find out because I need to get to class," says Valentina, moving back to the doorway.

"Yeah, we already had three pop quizzes today, and I don't want to take the chance on missing out on anything," agrees Chloe, following her.

"Sorry, Sophie, but my parents would kill me if they found out I was skipping something to do secret Santa research, so I'd better leave too," Mariama adds.

I shrug my shoulders. Now that I know my secret Santa is not Nathan or Toby, I'm determined to find out who he or she really is.

"I don't mind if I miss," says Nathan, pulling up a wooden chair beside me. "My last two classes are electives, art and P.E."

"The professor is taking a chance on skipping a subject?" laughs Toby. "This I gotta see. Of course, I know why you want to miss P.E. today, we are doing a unit on basketball!"

"Wait a minute now..." Nathan begins.

"Would you two please stop bickering and help get this done so maybe we don't have to miss class?" I hiss.

"Need any help over there, kids?" Mrs. Granger, our school librarian, peers over at us from above her cat-eyed glasses.

"No, ma'am," I answer and turn back to the monitor and type 'Westmeyer Girls' Center Houston.'

"How are you going to figure this out?" asks Toby as I click through the website. "There are probably hundreds of kids there, and I'm sure they wouldn't list individual pictures or names in case some creeper was trying to get them or something."

"Wait a minute, look at that girl!" Nathan points at a snapshot showing children with members of the Houston Texans football team. "She looks familiar, doesn't she? I know her from somewhere."

"It's Lanie Mitchell!" I exclaim, zooming in on the photo. "The bully who got kicked out of Xavier last year!"

"She stays in a girls' home?" asks Toby. "I thought you all told me she lived with her grandma."

"She did, but I guess she moved to the girls' home somehow. She looks so happy in these pictures!"

Lanie's face is lit up with a smile. When she was in our class at Xavier she scowled most of the time.

"Maybe things are better for her there," says Nathan.

"We've got to find a way to go see Lanie!" I exclaim.

"And just how do you plan to do that?" asks Toby. "Westmeyer is way farther than a scooter ride away. Will your parents drive you across town on a Friday night to meet your secret Santa?"

Toby has a point. I stop to think, and then I come up with the perfect solution. "I know who can take us…Granny Washington!"

Chapter 15

Driving Miss Sophie

"Drive you and your friend to a foster home to find your secret Santa?!" Granny Washington exclaims. "I'm not sure about that."

"But this is the perfect time for us to find out, Granny," I beg. "It's the Friday before winter break, so we don't have school tomorrow or homework to do and since Mom and Dad are staying late at the dental office for their holiday party, we'll be home before they are!"

"I thought Granny was taking us to Mega Burger for dinner after school!" Cole pouts.

"We can still go there, Cole, and maybe my Santa will have a gift for you, too." He settles down.

Toby and my other friends went home after school, but Nathan texted his parents that I invited him to hang out with our family for a few hours.

"Please, Granny! We have to find out who our Santa is!" I plead. "We think it's a girl who used to be in our class, and she's been sending Nathan presents too. We just want to thank whoever it is. You used to be a news reporter, Granny. This would be like getting a scoop on an exciting news story."

"Oh, all right," Granny says, giving in. "I guess it wouldn't hurt to drive by the place as long as we don't stay too long. I would like to figure out who your Santa is before Christmas."

"Come on, Nathan!" We quickly pile in the car before Granny changes her mind.

I get in the front seat and Nathan takes the back with Cole. Granny types the address we give her in the car's GPS navigation system.

"The girls' center is about ten miles from here," she says. "We'll get there in about fifteen minutes."

I settle in my seat and smile as she pulls out of the school parking lot.

Cole is happy because Nathan laughs at all his corny jokes.

"What do snowmen eat for breakfast?"

"What?" asks Nathan.

"Frosted flakes!"

"Where do snowmen go to dance?"

Nathan stares at him and shrugs his shoulder.

"A snow ball."

"Granny, make him stop!" I beg.

"You're the one who wanted to go for a longer car ride instead of out to eat," giggles Cole. "What do you get when you cross a snowman with a vampire?"

"Hold on, I know," interrupts Nathan, "Frost-bite!"

I tune out the comedy show and look out the window. I'm really getting excited. In just a few minutes, the mystery will be solved.

I'm impressed with how well Nathan does with Cole. He really listens to him.

"I wonder what kind of clouds those big fluffy ones are?" my brother asks.

"They are called cumulous," Nathan responds. I didn't know the answer, but even if I did I probably would have told Cole to Google it.

"I guess this is it," says Granny as we pull up to a large, three-story brick building.

"It looks more like an office than a place where orphans live," says Cole.

I know I wouldn't want to live here. Westmeyer Home for Girls' looks like a hospital. It reminds me of the time when my family had to sleep in Dad's office for safety during a hurricane because our house was in danger of flooding.

"Let's go to the front desk and see if we can visit with your friend," suggests Granny after we park the car.

Now I feel nervous. What are we going to say to Lanie?

"What if she doesn't want to see us?" asks Nathan.

"Well, we've come this far," says Granny. "Let's go in and find out."

Chapter 16

The Big Reveal

"We are visitors for Lanie Mitchell," I shyly say to the gray-haired, wrinkled, receptionist at the front desk after we enter the building.

"What is your relation to her?" she asks.

"We are old school friends," Nathan replies.

"Let me see if she's on the playground," the receptionist replies, picking up the phone at her desk. "The girls don't get many visitors, so this will be a nice treat."

Just like the outside, the inside of this place reminds me of Dad's dental office, minus the giant statue of a tooth. It is empty and scary looking, and not comfortable at all. The walls are a dingy, gray, and the cold steel-colored floor tile looks like it needs to be cleaned. A teenaged girl wearing too-short jeans and a faded tee shirt walks down the hall and stares at us curiously. A janitor in headphones sweeps up dust in a corner. I can't imagine leaving home to live in a place like this. I feel sorry for Lanie.

When she was at Xavier, she was mean to us and stole our lunch money and even knocked

Nathan down so he had knee surgery and was on crutches for a month, but I still wouldn't wish this on her.

The front desk attendant is still calling around to find out where Lanie is. We wait quietly for about five minutes, and my stomach starts to growl.

"Do you think they have snacks here?" whispers Cole.

"Just be patient," says Grandma.

Maybe this was a bad idea. Nathan seems content to flip through some old scouting magazines. Cole looks over his shoulder and rattles off more silly questions.

"Have you ever been camping? Would you like to go one day?"

After what seems like forever, the back door opens and Lanie walks in with a thin, blonde-haired lady. She looks a little shorter than I remember her being last year, but maybe that's because I've grown some. Lanie appears skinner, too. I hope they don't feed her gruel like they eat in that book *Oliver Twist*.

She scans around the room and then sees us. Her eyes widen. "Sophie, Nathan...w-what are you all doing here?"

"We came to thank our secret Santa," says Nathan, walking up to meet her.

"It's you, isn't it?" I ask.

Lanie stares at the floor for a minute and then moves her head up and down.

"How did you find out?" she asks. I explain about the flyer in the bottom of one of the gift boxes as Lanie wrings her hands and sways back and forth.

"Sending those gifts was very sweet of you, Lanie," says Granny Washington, patting her on the shoulder. "And very much in keeping with the holiday spirit."

"I hope you liked them," Lanie speaks quickly. "My mom sends me money every Thanksgiving to buy Christmas gifts since she doesn't come see me too often. I felt really badly about all those things I did to everybody at Xavier last year. My counselor said using the money to help those I hurt might be a way for me to forgive myself. I figured you might throw away something that came from me, so I decided to become your secret Santa."

I can't believe my ears. Lanie was just awful to us when she was in our class at Xavier. I never imagined her caring about what she had done.

"I'm not going to lie, I didn't like you too much last year," says Nathan, holding up his wrist to show his new bracelet. "But I do like the gifts you sent me. Thanks."

"I'm so glad you are not permanently hurt from me knocking you down, Nathan." Lanie starts to tear up. "Thanks for accepting my gifts."

"I'm sorry you have to live here, Lanie," I say. "Where is your grandma?"

"She got sick when I was at Xavier and started forgetting things. Some days she couldn't even cook dinner," Lanie explains. "Since Grammy couldn't take care of me anymore, they put her in a nursing home and had me come live here. I don't have any other family I could go live with and my parents don't want me."

Ms. Gimble, the lady who brought out Lanie, hugs her. "I'm Lanie's counselor. She was a very angry young lady when she first came to live with us here at Westmeyer, but she's made a lot of progress. She's doing wonderfully in school and made many new friends. Lanie feels terribly for the hurt she caused you children. I hope you can forgive her."

"Thanks so much for the gingerbread house and all the other nice gifts," I say.

"My favorite was the candy," Cole pipes up. "But the next time, don't worry about sending girly jewelry."

Everyone laughs.

"Well, we had better head home now to beat the traffic," Granny says. "Thanks so much, Ms. Gimble, for allowing the children to formally show their appreciation to Lanie, and Merry Christmas."

"Merry Christmas," we all say as we turn to leave.

"Wow, that was an even bigger surprise than I expected," says Nathan.

"Yeah, who'd have thought Lanie would be our secret Santa or that she'd be actually living in an orphanage?" I answer.

"I'm glad Lanie seems to be doing well despite all her challenges," says Granny. "Her situation should remind us all to appreciate all our blessings."

"Yeah, Sophie, I'm glad I just have to live with you and not a whole building of icky girls!" says Cole.

"I'm glad I have to live with you too, Cole." I turn to my brother and smile.

Chapter 17

Knock Out

We drop Nathan off at his house and decide to order pizza at home rather than go to Mega Burger.

"Come on, Cole, let's go outside," I tell my brother after we finish eating.

Cole and I head outside to shoot some hoops on his goal, and Bertram bounds out after us. After playing Knockout with Toby and his brother Michael the other day, I feel like I might be able to get good at this game. I shoot the ball to the basket and it bounces off the rim.

"Dang it!" I stomp my foot.

"Remember how Toby taught you to shoot last time, Sophie?" coaches Cole. "Follow through with your wrists when you let go of the ball, like this."

Grrrr...

Not five minutes after we've been outside, our dog starts growling.

"Oh no, just what we don't need," says Cole, still dribbling the ball. "Rhythm Jones."

Our neighbor trudges down the sidewalk and approaches our driveway.

"Hey, Pull Up!" I call out. "Want to challenge us in a game?"

"What are you doing, Sophie?" Cole whispers.

"Don't call me that," Rhythm warns.

"You're probably just scared we'll beat you," I tease.

"Oh yeah, I can beat you, your brother, and your dog with my eyes closed," Rhythm counters.

"Let's see what you got, kid," I say, bounce-passing him the ball. Rhythm steps up to our driveway.

For the next fifteen minutes we play Knockout, a game where players practice making free throws and lay ups, and the team who gets the most shots in wins. Cole and I are not doing too well because I am terrible at making my shots.

"Come on, Sophie. Get it in this time, just do what I taught you," my brother urges.

Rhythm laughs as my attempt at a free throw shot goes over the entire goal and bounces onto the brick wall of the house.

Cole retrieves the ball and shots a three pointer that swishes through the net.

"Nice!" Rhythm shakes his head in appreciation. Soon Blu joins us, and the three boys start having fun playing together. I sit down and scratch Bertram's back.

My parents drive up into the driveway.

"Good game, Cole," says Blu. "Maybe we can get you some practice another time."

"Yeah, you're not so bad for a 'Bougie Boy,'" Rhythm adds.

"All right 'Pull-Up,'" says Cole, laughing. "See you later."

"See you!" Rhythm gives Cole a fist bump, and he and Blu head back down the block toward their house.

"What was that all about?" Dad asks. "Aren't those the boys who were over here fighting the other day?"

"It's the funniest thing, Daddy," says Cole. "Rhythm started out being mean again but then Sophie called him over and got him to play with us."

"That's wonderful!" Mom exclaims. "How'd you do it?"

"I don't know," I said. "I thought about how their father doesn't come around much and kind of felt sorry for them. Sometimes if people don't have things so easy, they are meaner to other people than they should be. I figured if we started joking around things would get better."

"Well, it looks like you were right," said my father, patting me on the back.

"Yeah, thanks, Sophie," says Cole, smiling. "We've just got to work on your jump shot so we can beat them next time."

"Sure thing, Squirt," I say, grabbing the ball.

Chapter 18

A Gift for Santa

When we go inside the house, we tell Mom and Dad about our visit to Lanie Mitchell at the girl's home.

"Who'd have thought it was her?" marvels Mom. "That girl was just terrible to you kids last year."

"I'm happy that she seems to be doing well," says Granny Washington. "It's a shame that the child's parents don't come to see her."

"It may be a good thing, depending upon what is going on in their lives," says Dad.

"Maybe I should get her a Christmas gift," I suggest.

"That would be a wonderful idea," says Granny Washington.

The next day we go shopping so Cole and I can buy gifts for our parents. I select a pretty scarf for my mother and a red tie for Dad. Cole gets mom a beautiful crystal bracelet and buys my father three pair of basketball shorts. When Granny Washington goes to the restroom, we sneak and buy her a coloring book set for grownups with colored pencils.

"Sophie!" I turn after I hear my name called and see my friends Chloe and Valentina. "What are you doing here?" I say.

"Do you need to ask?" Cole grumbles. "Those two are always at the mall."

"We are getting our last-minute shopping gifts," says Valentina.

While my friends and I catch up, Granny takes Cole to the food court to get a hot pretzel. I tell them about our visit to the girls' home.

"That is so crazy that she lives there!" says Chloe. "She was so mean last year. But I do feel bad that she isn't with her family."

"I want to get Lanie a Christmas gift, but I'm not sure what to buy her," I say.

"What about a new outfit?" Valentina suggests.

"That's a great idea!" I say, remembering the too small clothes I saw one of the girls wearing at the orphanage.

We tell Granny Washington when she comes back with Cole, and she agrees that clothing would make a nice present so we head to one of Chloe's favorite clothing shops.

"This looks about her size," I say, holding up a cute hot pink and black-checked skirt. "And here is a black sweater that matches it perfectly."

"I'll buy these to go with it." Chloe selects a glittery headband and a pretty necklace that has a letter "L" charm.

"You guys as so sweet!" Valentina exclaims.

"Can we go home now?" Cole has finished his pretzel and is getting antsy.

"This should fit, but let's get a gift receipt in case she needs to exchange it for a different size," suggests Grandma.

The store clerk wraps the present for us. I feel great to be able to buy my Santa a special gift now that her secret is out.

"Merry Christmas, guys!" I say, giving my friends hugs as we get ready to leave the mall.

"Merry Christmas, Sophie! See you soon!" call Chloe and Valentina.

"Can we drop the present off to Lanie?" I ask.

"I don't see why not," Granny says.

"Ah, man! I wanted to get home to play my video game!" grumbles Cole.

"You can play later, young man," answers Grandma. "Now, let's go."

Once we arrive at the girls' home, I rush to the front desk with Lanie's present.

"Back so soon?" smiles the receptionist. "And I see you come bearing gifts."

"It's for my friend, Lanie Mitchell," I answer. "Is she here?"

"I believe they are having a little holiday celebration in the back," says the receptionist. "Let me see if it's all right to buzz you in."

"Follow me," she says after speaking with someone on the other line. "She leads us to a small room to the left of the front entrance. "This is the recreation center," she says.

"Sophie!" Lanie runs over from a group of girls she is standing by. She is wearing a Santa hat on her head.

"I brought this present for you, Lanie. Merry Christmas!"

"Thanks so much, Sophie," Lanie says, blushing and setting the package under a large Christmas tree in the corner. "Let me introduce you to some of my friends."

Grandma nods her head that it's okay, and Cole looks happy because the receptionist offers him cookies and hot apple cider.

"Not too much or you'll get a stomachache," cautions Grandma.

Lanie's friends seem pretty normal and nice. They talk about the work they are doing in their school and how they are happy it's vacation time. Some of them say they are going to visit family for the holidays.

"Ms. Gimble is having me come to her house for Christmas," says Lanie. "She has a niece our age named Bridgett, who is really nice, who will be there, so I'm excited about that."

"I'm glad you will have a happy Christmas, Lanie," I say smiling.

"All right, everyone, gather around!" calls one of the teachers. "We are going to sing some Christmas carols." She passes out slips of paper with the lyrics on them. Somebody hands Granny Washington, Cole, and me lyric sheets and gives us Santa hats to put on.

Piano music starts and we all begin to sing:

> *Hark the herald angels sing*
> *"Glory to the newborn King!*
> *Peace on earth and mercy mild*
> *God and sinners reconciled"*
> *Joyful, all ye nations rise*
> *Join the triumph of the skies*
> *With the angelic host proclaim:*
> *"Christ is born in Bethlehem"*
> *Hark! The herald angels sing*
> *"Glory to the newborn King!"*

Merry Christmas Everyone!

Dear Reader:

Thank you for reading *Sophie Washington: Secret Santa*, a Sophie Washington holiday special! I hope you liked it. If you enjoyed the book, I'd be grateful if you post a short review on Amazon. Your feedback really makes a difference and helps others learn about my books. I appreciate your support!

Tonya

P.S. Please visit my website at www.tonyaduncanellis.com to see cool videos about Sophie and learn about upcoming books (I sometimes give away freebies!). You can also join Sophie's club to get updates about my new book releases and get a **FREE** gift.

Books by
Tonya Duncan Ellis

For information on all Tonya Duncan Ellis books about Sophie and her friends

Check out the following pages!

You'll find:

• Blurbs about the other exciting books in the Sophie Washington series

• Information about Tonya Duncan Ellis

Sophie Washington: Queen of the Bee

Sign up for the spelling bee?

No way!

If there's one thing ten-year-old Texan Sophie Washington is good at, it's spelling. She's earned straight one-hundreds on all her spelling tests to prove it. Her parents want her to compete in the Xavier Academy spelling bee, but Sophie wishes they would buzz off.

Her life in the Houston suburbs is full of adventures, and she doesn't want to slow down the action. Where else can you chase wild hogs out of your yard, ride a bucking sheep or spy an eight-foot-long alligator during a bike ride through the neighborhood? Studying spelling words seems as fun as getting stung by a hornet, in comparison.

That's until her irritating classmate, Nathan Jones, challenges her. There's no way she can let Mr. Know-it-All win. Studying is hard when you have a pesky younger brother and a busy social calendar. Can Sophie ignore the distractions and become Queen of the Bee?

Sophie Washington:
The Snitch

There's nothing worse than being a tattletale...

That's what ten-year-old Sophie Washington thinks until she runs into Lanie Mitchell, a new girl at school. Lanie pushes Sophie and her friends around at their lockers and even takes their lunch money.

If they tell, they are scared the other kids in their class will call them snitches and won't be their friends. And when you're in the fifth grade, nothing seems worse than that. Excitement at home keeps Sophie's mind off the trouble with Lanie.

She takes a fishing trip to the Gulf of Mexico with her parents and little brother, Cole, and discovers a mysterious creature in the attic above her room. For a while, Sophie is able to keep her parents from knowing what is going on at school. But Lanie's bullying goes too far, and a classmate gets seriously hurt. Sophie needs to make a decision. Should she stand up to the bully or become a snitch?

Sophie Washington: Things You Didn't Know About Sophie

Oh, the tangled web we weave...

Sixth grader Sophie Washington thought she had life figured out when she was younger, but this school year everything changed. She feels like an outsider because she's the only one in her class without a cell phone, and her crush, new kid Toby Johnson, has been calling her best friend Chloe. To fit in, Sophie changes who she is. Her plan to become popular works for a while, and she and Toby start to become friends.

Between the boy drama, Sophie takes a whirlwind class field trip to Austin, Texas, where she visits the state museum, eats Tex-Mex food, and has a wild ride on a kayak. Back at home, Sophie fights off buzzards from her family's roof, dissects frogs in science class, and has fun at her little brother Cole's basketball tournament.

Things get more complicated when Sophie "borrows" a cell phone and gets caught. If her parents make her tell the truth what will her friends think? Turns out Toby has also been hiding something, and Sophie discovers the best way to make true friends is to be yourself.

Sophie Washington: The Gamer

40 Days Without Video Games? Oh No!

Sixth-grader Sophie Washington and her friends are back with an interesting book about having fun with video games while keeping balance. It's almost Easter, and Sophie and her family get ready to start fasts for Lent with their church, where they give up doing something for forty days that may not be good for them. Her parents urge Sophie to stop tattling so much and encourage her second-grade brother, Cole, to give up something he loves most—playing video games. The kids agree to the challenge but how long can they keep it up? Soon after Lent begins, Cole starts sneaking to play his video games. Things start to get out of control when he loses a school electronic tablet he checked out without his parents' permission and comes to his sister for help. Should Sophie break her promise and tattle on him?

Sophie Washington: Hurricane

#Sophie Strong

A hurricane's coming, and eleven-year-old Sophie Washington's typical middle school life in the Houston, Texas suburbs is about to make a major change. One day she's teasing her little brother, Cole, dodging classmate Nathan Jones' wayward science lab frog and complaining about "braggamuffin" cheerleader Valentina Martinez, and the next, she and her family are fleeing for their lives to avoid dangerous flood waters. Finding a place to stay isn't easy during the disaster, and the Washington's get some surprise visitors when they finally do locate shelter. To add to the trouble, three members of the Washington family go missing during the storm, and new friends lose their home. In the middle of it all, Sophie learns to be grateful for what she has and that she is stronger than she ever imagined.

Sophie Washington: Mission: Costa Rica

Welcome to the Jungle

Sixth grader Sophie Washington, her good friends, Chloe and Valentina, and her parents and brother, Cole, are in for a week of adventure when her father signs them up for a spring break mission trip to Costa Rica. Sophie has dreams of lazing on the beach under palm trees, but these are squashed quicker than an underfoot banana once they arrive in the rainforest and are put to work, hauling buckets of water, painting and cooking. Near the hut they sleep in, the girls fight off wayward iguanas and howler monkeys, and nightly visits from a surprise "guest" make it hard for them to get much rest after their work is done.

A wrong turn in the jungle midway through the week makes Sophie wish she could leave South America and join another classmate who is doing a spring break vacation in Disney World.

Between the daily chores the family has fun times zip lining through the rainforest and taking an exciting river cruise in crocodile-filled waters. Sophie meets new friends during the mission week who show her a different side of life, and by the end of the trip she starts to see Costa Rica as a home away from home.

About the Author

Tonya Duncan Ellis is author of the Sophie Washington book series which includes: *Queen of the Bee, The Snitch, Things You Didn't Know About Sophie, The Gamer, Hurricane, Mission: Costa Rica,* and *Secret Santa.* When she's not writing, she enjoys reading, swimming, biking and travel. Tonya lives in Houston, TX with her husband and three children.